Written By
Denise Leduc

Illustrated By
Breanne Taylor

Poppies, Poppies Everywhere! by Denise Leduc

Illustrations by Breanne Taylor

Published by Lilac Arch Press
Saskatchewan, Canada
www.lilacarchpress.com

LILAC
ARCH PRESS

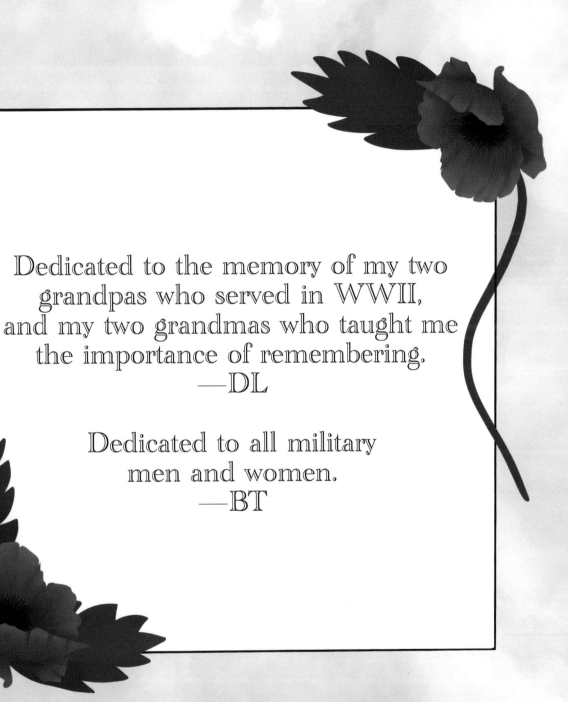

Dedicated to the memory of my two
grandpas who served in WWII,
and my two grandmas who taught me
the importance of remembering.
—DL

Dedicated to all military
men and women.
—BT

On a frosty November day, Charlotte strolled through the park with Grandma. She spotted a colourful playground. It had monkey bars and slides, her two favourite things!

"Can we go? Can we go?" Charlotte asked.

Grandma shook her head.
"Not today," she said. "We have
something special to do today."

Charlotte pouted.

She trudged through the
damp leaves.
Why couldn't she go play?
She kicked at the leaves.

"Come along," said Grandma

At the other side of the park Grandma stopped at a table. A man and woman wearing uniforms sat there. Grandma talked to them. She was smiling and her eyes twinkled.

Charlotte was about to stomp her foot. She stopped when she saw Grandma put money in a box and pull out two pretty red flowers. She looked in Grandma's hand and saw they weren't real. They were soft to the touch and had a small pin in the middle.

Grandma pinned one flower on her fleece coat. Then, she pinned the other on Charlotte's purple coat. Charlotte still felt mad about missing the playground, but she remembered these flowers from school.

Grandma said, "This is a poppy. You wear it close to your heart."

A big gust of wind chilled the air, so Charlotte and Grandma went inside for a hot chocolate.

"What are poppies for, again, Grandma?" Charlotte asked.

"They're for Remembrance Day,"Grandma answered. "Remembrance Day is every November 11th. We remember the soldiers and veterans who went to war to give us freedom."

"Today is Remembrance Day. We will go to a ceremony to show we care."

Charlotte thought a ceremony sounded B-O-R-I-N-G. That playground would be so much more fun.

As they reached the centre of town they followed the quiet chatter of the crowd.

People lined up along the street. Charlotte and Grandma found a place to stand.

A parade of soldiers and veterans marched tall and proud in their uniforms. Some looked like moms and dads, and some looked older than Grandma. A very old man in a wheelchair waved. Many people in the parade wore medals on their chest.
.

Charlotte touched the poppy on her coat.

A band played a marching song.
Charlotte liked the big drums.
She tapped her feet to the beat.

Charlotte saw some Canadian flags.
A friendly kid standing close by had two
flags. He gave one to Charlotte. Now,
she could have her own flag as
the parade marched by.

1914 - 1918

IN SERVICE TO CANADA   AU SERVICE DU CANADA

THE UNKNOWN   LE SOLDAT
SOLDIER   INCONNU

After the parade, everyone gathered around a towering stone statue showing soldiers and the dates 1914-1918.

Charlotte counted the soldiers on the statue, 1, 2, 3...

She knew they weren't real, but they looked like they could have been real people. She thought about the soldiers and what it would be like to leave your home and family. It must be scary.

She touched the poppy on her coat again. She looked around. She liked that everyone was wearing a poppy.

The mayor stood at a podium and talked into the microphone. Everyone was suddenly so quiet you could hear leaves rustle on the breeze.

The band began to play again.
The crowd sang, "O Canada".

Next, a teenage boy in a cadet uniform went to the stage to read the poem, "In Flanders Fields". Charlotte had heard it before in school.

One by one different clergy members stood at the podium and shared prayers. Lots of people bowed their heads. Charlotte did too.

After the final prayer a soldier took
out a shiny gold instrument.
"That's a bugle," Grandma whispered.
The soldier played a slow, sad tune.
Charlotte squeezed Grandma's warm hand.

The clock struck eleven. As the chimes
rang out loud and clear through the cold
November air a deeper hush fell over
the crowd. Again, some people bowed
their heads. Others had a tear or two
shimmer on their cheeks.

Everyone stayed quiet,
for two whole minutes.

When the silence ended, some people laid wreaths by the statue. There were poppies, poppies everywhere!

"The poppies bring us all together," Charlotte whispered.

Grandma smiled

As they left Remembrance Day service, Charlotte waved at an elderly man in a uniform. He waved back and paused.

Still holding Grandma's hand, Charlotte said, "Thank you."

A gentle smile crossed the old man's face. "I like your poppy," he said pointing to the red flower on her coat.

Charlotte and Granda were quiet as they walked back through the park.

Charlotte looked up at Grandma. "I like my poppy too," she said. "I really do."

Questions for Discussion

When was the first Remembrance Day?

Why is the number eleven important to Remembrance Day?

Remembrance Day services might look different in different places. How does your community honour Remembrance Day?

What other countries observe Remembrance Day?

Why do you think it is a good idea to observe Remembrance Day

Why are we silent for two whole minutes?

What is the difference between a soldier and a veteran?

What is a cadet?

What song was played on the bugle?

Remembrance Day Activities

-Make a poppy craft

-Talk to your family about relatives who may have served in the military

-Find and learn a Remembrance Day poem

-Make up your own Remembrance Day poem

-Write to members serving in the Canadian Armed Forces

-Thank a veteran

-Visit a war memorial or museum

-Attend a Remembrance Day service

-Pause for two minutes of silence on Remembrance Day

Denise Leduc is a Canadian writer who was born and raised in Sarnia, Ontario. She currently resides in rural Saskatchewan. She writes fiction, non-fiction, poetry, and children's books. Her love of books also had her pursue degrees in English and work as a librarian. She is the founder of Prairie Bear Books, a registered charity dedicated to bringing books to children and youth through community partnerships
www.prairiebearbooks.org

Breanne Taylor lives in Louisiana where she work full-time as a law enforcement officer. She has a passion for illustrating children's books. To see more of her illustrations she can be found on Instagram
@bt.illustrate

Printed in Great Britain
by Amazon

31084321R00021